ARE YOU FEELING SILLY ENOUGH TO READ MORE?

My Brother's Famous Bottom
MY DAD'S GOT AN ALLIGATOR!
MY GRANNY'S GREAT ESCAPE
MY MUM'S GOING TO EXPLODE!
MY BROTHER'S FAMOUS BOTTOM
MY BROTHER'S FAMOUS BOTTOM GETS PINCHED
MY BROTHER'S FAMOUS BOTTOM GOES CAMPING
MY BROTHER'S HOT CROSS BOTTOM
MY BROTHER'S CHRISTMAS BOTTOM – UNWRAPPED!
MY BROTHER'S FAMOUS BOTTOM GETS CROWNED!
MY BROTHER'S FAMOUS BOTTOM TAKES OFF!

The Hundred-mile-an-hour Dog
THE HUNDRED-MILE-AN-HOUR DOG
RETURN OF THE HUNDRED-MILE-AN-HOUR DOG
CHRISTMAS CHAOS FOR THE HUNDRED-MILE-AN-HOUR DOG
WANTED! THE HUNDRED-MILE-AN-HOUR DOG
LOST! THE HUNDRED-MILE-AN-HOUR DOG
THE HUNDRED-MILE-AN-HOUR DOG GOES FOR GOLD!
KIDNAPPED! THE HUNDRED-MILE-AN-HOUR DOG'S SIZZLING SUMMER
THE HUNDRED-MILE-AN-HOUR DOG: MASTER OF DISGUISE

Cartoon Kid
CARTOON KID – SUPERCHARGED!
CARTOON KID STRIKES BACK!
CARTOON KID – EMERGENCY!
CARTOON KID – ZOMBIES!

Cosmic Pyjamas
DOCTOR BONKERS!
KRANKENSTEIN'S CRAZY HOUSE OF HORROR

AND EVEN MORE?

THE BEAK SPEAKS
BEWARE! KILLER TOMATOES
FATBAG: THE DEMON VACUUM CLEANER
INVASION OF THE CHRISTMAS PUDDINGS
ROMANS ON THE RAMPAGE!

JEREMY STRONG'S LAUGH-YOUR-SOCKS-OFF JOKE BOOK
JEREMY STRONG'S LAUGH-YOUR-SOCKS-OFF EVEN MORE JOKE BOOK

THE KING OF COMEDY

Jeremy STRONG

The Hundred-Mile An-Hour Dog

MASTER OF DISGUISE

Illustrated by Rowan Clifford

PUFFIN

PUFFIN BOOKS

UK | USA | Canada | Ireland | Australia
India | New Zealand | South Africa

Puffin Books is part of the Penguin Random House group of companies
whose addresses can be found at global.penguinrandomhouse.com.

puffinbooks.com

Penguin
Random House
UK

First published 2016
001

Text copyright © Jeremy Strong, 2016
Illustrations copyright © Rowan Clifford, 2016

The moral right of the author and illustrator has been asserted

Set in Baskerville MT
Printed in Great Britain by Clays Ltd, St Ives plc

A CIP catalogue record for this book is available from the British Library

ISBN: 978–0–141–36143–7

www.greenpenguin.co.uk

This is for HMRC

Contents

1. Rabbits!

Streaker is the speediest dog in the world. She can run faster than a bullet overtaking another bullet. She runs ALL the time, even when she's sleeping. She lies on my bed at night, snoring, and her whiskers are twitching, her ears are flicking and her legs are going gallopy gallop gallop. Sometimes her legs are running so much she actually moves along the bed and ends up sitting on my head like a gigantic dog-shaped hat.

Everyone in my house is pretty sporty. Streaker is always galloping. Mum is always cycling, or running, or swimming, or exercising. As for Dad, he's always playing golf, but is that a sport? Really? All you do is wander about and hit things from time to time or look for them. Dad spends most of his time hunting for his golf balls. That's because he keeps hitting them into the trees, ponds and bunkers that cover the golf course.

Or maybe it's because when Streaker finds them she tries to eat them and then she's sick. Urrgh. Then WHO gets into trouble? Me. ME! Did I eat Dad's golf balls? No. Was I sick on the carpet? No. But you see whenever Streaker causes a problem I'm the one that gets the blame because Streaker is MY dog. That's what Dad says.

'She's your dog, Trevor. You clear up the mess.'

'But Dad, you decided we had to have a dog. You bought her and told us she was the family dog.'

'Yes, I did, Trevor. You're quite right. She is the family dog and it's your family job to look after her. Now go and clear up that dog sick.'

Huh. I can't win, can I? What's more I'm supposed to take Streaker for walks. That's what Dad says. Well, you can't just WALK Streaker. Streaker doesn't WALK anywhere. She runs. She dashes. She whizzes. At full speed. *Swoooosh!* She's the fastest dog on the planet. In fact, she's probably the fastest dog in the universe.

So here we are in the middle of the Easter school break and I've got to walk Streaker because everyone else is busy. When I say 'everyone else' I mean Mum and Dad and when I say 'busy' I mean Dad is out playing golf and Mum is tinkering with her new bike. Sigh. My mum and her bikes. Let me explain.

Mum has just bought herself a racing bike. Maybe I should tell you that she already has two mountain bikes.

'You've got to keep fit, Trev,' she pants, halfway through doing thirty press-ups.

'I do keep fit, Mum. I have to walk Streaker. Remember? That means running everywhere. Anyhow, why do you need a new bike?'

Mum grinned up at me. 'Triathlon. I'm taking part in one.'

I had to ask. 'What's a triathlon?'

'It's a special race. You have to do three things – swim, ride and run. You wear a special suit that means you don't have to change. First you swim, then you jump on your bike, pedal like mad, jump off and run the final bit to the finish line.'

'Sounds mad,' I suggested. 'Why would anyone want to do that?'

Mum's grin got bigger. 'Exercise, Trev, exercise. You don't want a baggy, wrinkly mum, do you?'

I shook my head, but really I don't care what Mum looks like. She's my mum and that's all there is to it. It's just like people say – you can choose your friends but you can't choose your family. You're stuck with them for the rest of your life – and never forget that they're stuck with you!

Anyway, I had a dog to walk so I decided to take Streaker up near the golf course. She likes it up there because there are lots of rabbits that she likes to chase. Luckily, there are also lots of holes for the rabbits to disappear down. You can almost hear them laughing: *Ha ha! We fooled that silly old dog. Fancy thinking she could catch us! Hee hee hee.* And then they all have a party to celebrate their escape and drink carrot juice and eat carrot cake and pop carrot-shaped balloons.

I put Streaker on the lead and headed up towards the footpath next to the golf course. When I say 'headed' I really meant that I was DRAGGED AT HIGH SPEED BY A DESPERATE DOG. (The desperate dog being Streaker of course.) Honestly, it's like being pulled along by a Ferrari with a tow bar. Streaker does this every time we go out. It's astonishing that I even managed to catch sight of the little posters stuck on all the lamp posts we passed.

MY DOG HAS BEEN STOLEN!

My dog, Pooper, was stolen from
outside the supermarket on Tuesday.

Please contact me if you have
any information.

£50 reward if successful.

Well, that was food for thought. What kind of person would call their dog Pooper? Even so, it's no fun having your dog stolen. You'd be pretty upset. Mind you, I couldn't imagine my dad coughing up fifty pounds to find Streaker. Nevertheless, it was a lot of money, the sort of money you might need to pay to have your arms stuck back on your body because your dog had just pulled them off.

'STREAKER! Why can't you just WALK?'

Does she listen? Of course not. She doesn't even turn round to see who's speaking. Her nose is pointing in one direction only and the rest of her is following. I spend most of my time trying to hold on to every passing lamp post, telephone pole, bush or front gate.

Anyhow, we got up to the fields and I let Streaker off her lead. *Zooooosh!* She was off like a rabbit-seeking missile. I simply stood there and watched as Streaker raced across that field, round it, criss-crossing it, until at last she spotted – THE RABBIT!

Quick! Warp Factor Five! Streaker's legs were a blur of speed. I almost expected to see her take off. The rabbit just sat there and watched. You'd better move, Mr Rabbit! Streaker's going to get you this time!

Streaker was charging at full pelt towards the rabbit and just when she was almost on top of it the rabbit disappeared down its hole, which it had been sitting right next to the entire time.

Mr Rabbit was definitely playing hide-and-seek because a moment later up he popped from another hole just a few metres away from where Streaker now had her nose buried down the first hole. I had to laugh. The rabbit was sitting right behind Streaker and watching, while Streaker kept pushing her nose uselessly into the hole.

At last she noticed Mr Rabbit, whirled round and, just as Streaker jumped, the rabbit popped

back down *that* hole and vanished. And so it

began all over again. Rabbits kept popping up

all over the field while Streaker dashed fruitlessly

after one, then another, then another. Or perhaps

they were all the same rabbit. Who knows? (Mr
Rabbit, probably!)

I got bored watching Streaker and turned to the golf course instead where several groups of players were wandering about, hunting for their golf balls. Then I saw Tina on the other side of the course. She was taking Mouse for a walk. (Mouse is actually a huge St Bernard. I guess you could say that Mouse is one big joke.)

OK, let's get this straight right away. Tina is my friend. She's a very good friend. I like her. She's clever and funny. She's a friend. Just that. She's not my GIRLfriend, OK? I know she says she is, but that's just her. I'm telling you she's not. And I know my mum and dad like to say she's my girlfriend, but she ISN'T. She's just a friend. Have I made that quite clear? Good. We only hold hands sometimes and that's only because she gets scared.

I waved across at her. Tina stopped and waved back. Mouse stopped and waved back. (No, of course he didn't! It was just his tongue doing a lot of flopping about.)

That was when Streaker spotted Mouse and

Mouse spotted Streaker. Now Streaker and
Mouse are best friends, a bit like me and Tina,
and I don't mean they hold paws with each other.
They're just always pleased to see each other.
So Streaker goes tearing across the golf course,
and Mouse goes plodding towards her, and when
they reach each other they happen to be right
beside one of those sandpit things you see on golf
courses. (They're called bunkers. Don't ask me
why. I think they should be called bonkers instead
of bunkers. Bonkers is a much better word for
something as daft as a sandpit in the middle of a
golf course.)

So Streaker and Mouse go rolling into the
bunker and start jumping on top of each other
and kicking the sand around and soon there's
sand going everywhere. The two dogs are
growling and leaping and rolling and shaking
their fur and having the best play fight ever when
all of a sudden – *PLOPPP!* A golf ball comes
whizzing out of nowhere and lands in the bunker.

The dogs take no notice and just carry on with their play fight. Then three golfers come along. Oh dear, one of them is my dad and, even worse, he's with Sergeant Smugg, our local policeman, and Mr Boffington-Orr, who is not only the Chief Constable but also president of the golf club.

Do they look happy? No, they don't.

'Get those wretched dogs out of that bunker!' yelled the Chief Constable. 'My ball is in there somewhere. We're midway through a game. Get those dogs *out*!'

'No dogs allowed!' bellowed Sergeant Smugg. 'Oi! I know that black one. That's Streaker! She's always causing trouble.'

My dad had turned white. Who could he blame? Oh, I know – ME!

'Trevor!' he yelled. 'Get the dogs out of there at once!'

I started to run towards the bunker, but there wasn't much point because Streaker had suddenly discovered the Chief Constable's ball and she was on it like a shot, grabbing it in her mouth and running off, with Mouse close behind her. Not far behind Mouse came two rabbits and then the Chief Constable and Sergeant Smugg. Dad just stood and watched in dismay. Oh dear. There's trouble ahead.

2. Boot Camp!

Did I say trouble? Trouble indeed. Dad was almost thrown out of the golf club for vandalism. (Ha ha! Dad – the vandal!) By the time he got home he was fuming.

'Vandalism!' he snorted. 'I wasn't doing anything. It was that pesky dog of yours, Trevor.'

Did you notice that? Did you see how all of a sudden Streaker was no longer the family dog? Oh no, definitely not, because Streaker was in trouble and that meant she was now MY dog. TREVOR'S dog. So I was in trouble too. Again.

'The vandal was Streaker,' Dad went on. 'Why can't you control her, Trevor?'

I wanted to ask Dad why HE couldn't control Streaker either. After all, he's a grown-up. Of course I didn't say anything because I knew it would get me into even more trouble and besides I knew the answer. Nobody can control Streaker. She just does whatever she wants. Sometimes it's something nice, like wagging her tail and resting her nose on your knee and looking at you adoringly, and sometimes it's the worst crime ever, like digging up bonkers, I mean bunkers, on golf courses.

Anyhow, Dad hadn't finished letting off steam and I knew it was best to wait until he'd come off the boil. Come on, Dad, get it all off your chest! And he did.

'I'm telling you, if that dog misbehaves just once more I'm sending her to boot camp.'

Eh? Boot camp? Isn't that for soldiers?

'But that's the army, Dad.'

'Not the boot camp I'm thinking of. It's for badly behaved dogs and it's near here. The dogs have a week of special hard-core training where they're taught how to behave properly. If they're not obedient by the end of the week they have to stay on for another week, and another, and another,' he added grimly.

Jumping jam pots! At that rate I'd never see Streaker again! This was serious. Streaker would HATE boot camp. I could see it now. She would try to escape. She'd succeed (because she's pretty smart even when she's acting stupid)

and she would probably never come back home afterwards. Why should she? Would you go back to a family that had just dumped you in prison for a week? Of course not.

'You can't send Streaker away,' I pleaded.

'Just watch me,' grunted Dad. 'I'm warning you, Trevor, one more incident like this morning and Streaker will be in that boot camp.'

So there we are. I know what Dad's like when he makes up his mind. He's like an elephant stuck in concrete. Immovable. It was time to send for the Special Emergency Services, also known as Tina. I put Streaker on the lead and let myself be pulled, yanked and have most of my bones pulled out of their joints by Streaker's efforts to reach Tina's house in record time. Streaker must have known it was an emergency.

'Are you all right?' asked Tina, as I stood panting on her doorstep. 'You look like something the dog's dragged all the way here and oh, look – there's the dog!'

'Oh, ha ha, I don't think,' I grunted because I was in a pretty bad mood. I think you would be too if you'd just had all your bones jiggled about by a mad canine.

'Cheer up,' Tina smiled. 'Come in and lie on the couch and tell me all your troubles and then I'll tell you where you went wrong.'

'How long have you been a psychiatrist?' I asked.

Tina beamed at me. 'As long as I've known you, Trevor.'

I ignored that unkind remark and went in. Streaker and Mouse were very happy to be reunited. At least they entertained each other, so Tina and I could talk. We sat upstairs on her bed and I spilled out my tale of raging fathers and boot camps and hysterical dogs, not to mention hysterical Trevors.

'That is a problem,' Tina agreed.

'I'm glad you think so. But how do we solve it?'

'Well, the obvious way is to keep Streaker out of trouble.'

'You know, Tina, I am ASTOUNDED that I never thought of that myself.'

Tina patted my knee. 'Sarcasm won't get you anywhere, young man.'

Honestly, now she was sounding like our head teacher.

'Tina, I have spent the last three YEARS trying to keep Streaker out of trouble. It doesn't work. All that happens is that I get dragged INTO trouble. At this rate I shall probably end up being sent to boot camp too. It will be Boot Camp for Dogs and Trevors.'

'Well, I'm glad you haven't lost your sense of humour,' laughed Tina, 'because that's what I like about you. And your good looks of course. You're quite handsome when you're not scowling.'

Tina snuggled up a bit closer to me. I edged away as far as I could without falling off the bed – unsuccessfully because I did fall off and lay there on the floor, looking rather stupid.

'There's no need for you to throw yourself at
my feet,' Tina grinned. 'You know I'm happy to
marry you.'

'We're eleven,' I reminded her.

'I can wait.'

'How about we work out a plan for Streaker
instead?' I suggested.

'Are you trying to change the subject?'

'Yes, I am. There are things to discuss that are
far more serious.'

'Marriage is a very serious subject,' Tina said.

'I'm talking about Streaker!'

'Oh, Trevor, chill out. I'm joking! OK, how about this? Let's say Streaker misbehaves again and your dad decides to ring the boot camp.'

'OK,' I agreed. 'What do I do?'

'Get Streaker out of the house as soon as possible, hopefully without your dad knowing. You'll have to bring her round here. I think Mum will be OK with that.'

I nodded. Tina's mum was pretty easy-going and had helped with Streaker before when she'd been in trouble with my parents.

'That's OK, but your mum won't want her to stay here forever,' I pointed out.

'Probably not, but maybe your dad will calm down after a few days and allow her back.'

'What if he doesn't?'

'Then we move on to Plan B,' said Tina.

'Which is –?'

'I have no idea. I was hoping you wouldn't ask.

But don't worry, we'll think about that if and when Plan A has failed.' Tina took hold of my hands and looked at me intently.

'Don't worry. Everything will be fine.'

I felt like I was being hypnotized. Tina's pale blue eyes stared back at me, full of – what? It was like her eyes were tubes of soothing lotion that were spreading calm all over me.

I felt myself give her hands a squeeze and heard myself say, 'Thanks, Tina,' and squeeze her hands again. Then I suddenly came to and hastily snatched my hands away. What was I doing? Holding hands! Squeezing? We'd be married in a week at this rate!

Phew, that had been a lucky escape. I got to my feet. 'I'm going back home now.'

'OK, but stay calm,' Tina suggested. 'I read in Mum's magazine that some psychiatrists think that dogs pick up on their owner's moods, so if you're a bit crazy then your dog will behave like that too.'

I stared at her. 'So now you're saying that Streaker only behaves like an idiot because I'm one too?'

Tina shrugged. 'It's not my idea. It was the psychiatrists who said it. Psychiatrists are very clever you know.'

I'm sure she was smirking.

'Really? So, when Mouse sits on the floor and sticks his back leg into one ear to have a good scratch, he's actually copying what you do?'

Tina glared at me. Ha ha! THAT stopped her smirking.

'You're a real smarty-pants today, aren't you, Trevor?'

24

I just smiled. OK – so it was a BIG triumphant smile. After all, it's not often I get the better of Tina, so I was enjoying the moment A LOT!

Tina sighed and we said goodbye to each other and Streaker said goodbye to Mouse, which basically meant trying to bite one of her ears. But then Mouse was trying to bite one of hers. I guess that meant Tina and I were supposed to be biting each other's ears too. NO WAY! If you ask me those mind doctors have got a lot to answer for.

On the way home Streaker actually walked quietly beside me for once and by the time I reached the house I was feeling a lot better and more upbeat. Streaker was behaving well and, if things changed and went wrong, then at least I could smuggle her over to Tina's.

I couldn't help thinking about what Tina had said as I left. So some psychiatrists thought that dogs copied the behaviour of their owner. I reckoned that was the biggest load of rubbish I had ever heard, and I was remembering how

Streaker had dragged me like some crazy idiot all the way to Tina's house. And then a light bulb went on in my head. Actually, it was more like a firework and I suddenly realized where those psychiatrists had gone wrong.

IT SHOULD BE THE OTHER WAY ROUND!

Dogs don't behave like their owners. Dogs make their owners behave like them! Streaker was crazy and she made me seem crazy because I was trying to control her! Ha ha! Those mind-doctor people haven't got a clue!

3. Everything is Pants

Streaker's been pretty good for the last couple of days, apart from stealing my underpants. She takes them off to her basket and sleeps on them. So that just proves how wrong those psychiatrists are. Have I been stealing her underpants? Of course not.

But this morning I did have a bit of a panic. I was lying in bed having a wash. In other words I was lying in bed and Streaker was on top of me, licking me all over, as she likes to do in the morning.

I heard Dad go to the bathroom. Then he went back to the bedroom. He was clumping about, getting dressed and grunting to himself. Drawers were pulled out and slammed shut. Wardrobe doors were opened and banged. I heard him talking to Mum and his voice was getting louder.

He was angry about something, but I knew it couldn't be Streaker because she was with me, so I felt quite safe. No boot camp for my dog.

Dad's voice got so loud that I could hear him from my bedroom.

'Where are my underpants? I can't find any underpants anywhere. Did you put them in the wash?'

I heard Mum say she hadn't done any such thing. She told him to take better care of his clothes.

'But they've all disappeared!' Dad shouted. 'Have we been burgled by an underpants robber?'

And that was when I sat up straight, frozen with horror. AN UNDERPANTS ROBBER! I KNEW WHO THAT WAS!

I leaped out of bed and crept downstairs.
There in the dog basket was a pile of Dad's
underpants. NOOOOOOO! What should I do?
I couldn't take them back up to Dad. He'd only
ask where I'd found them. On the other hand
I had to get them out of the dog basket and
put them somewhere. So I shoved them in the
washing machine and left one pair hanging half
out, as a big clue.

I crept back to my room and I was only just
in time too because Dad came storming out
and started thumping about the house, shouting
about underpants and robbers. I think he was
even threatening to call the police, but luckily
Mum went to the kitchen to make him a nice
calming cup of tea and she caught sight of the
washing machine.

I must say she was rather puzzled.

'How did that happen? I don't remember
putting all your pants in the machine.'

Dad gave her a dark look. 'You must have.

I asked you if you'd put them in the wash and there they are. You're going crazy.'

'But I didn't put them there,' insisted Mum.

'It's all the cycling and running and swimming you're doing. It's turned your brain into mush and you have no idea what you're doing any longer. Look, you've just put two tea bags in the jam pot and now you're pouring hot water on them.'

Mum's eyes flew wide open and she clapped a hand to her head. 'It's you!' she shouted. 'Yelling at me about pant robbers and all that nonsense! I was paying attention to you and not to what I was doing.'

Mum rescued the tea bags and the jam and started making tea and breakfast all over again while Dad went upstairs with an armful of underpants and I heaved a sigh of relief. So did Streaker. She gave me her special look. The one that says THANK YOU!

At breakfast Dad announced that he was going

to start decorating the back room. He and Mum had been planning it for a few weeks and Dad was going to do all the wallpapering, with Mum's help. However, first of all Dad had to play several golf matches. (In other words he was putting off the decorating.) That could have gone on for quite a while, but Mum got tired of waiting and hid Dad's golf clubs and said he couldn't have them until the room was papered.

So Dad was really going to start now. I thought it would be a good time to get out of the house in case I got lumbered with the decorating too, so I fetched Streaker and set off for Tina's so we could walk the dogs together.

'How are things?' Tina asked, as we walked up the street. (That's to say Tina walked with Mouse while I was dragged and yanked and pulled apart by Streaker.) I told Tina about Dad and the underpants and the decorating.

'Wallpapering is fun,' Tina told me.

'Yeah?'

'You have to make up a big bucketful of really gloopy wallpaper paste. Mum and I did her bedroom a few months ago. It's difficult to get the paper up sometimes, but putting the paste on is really fun. I pasted the wallpaper and then Mum put it up.'

Just at that moment we saw Charlie Smugg on the other side of the street. He was walking his three Alsatians and had a couple of friends with him. At least that was what I thought, but Tina told me something different.

'That's his gang,' she whispered.

'Charlie's got a gang?'

'Yes, and guess what they're called?'

'Tell me!'

'Charlie's Gang.'

'Yes, you told me, but what are they called?' I asked.

'That's it,' said Tina. 'They're called Charlie's Gang. So original, don't you think?'

We both laughed. 'He's an idiot,' I said.

'Yeah, an idiot with a gang,' murmured Tina. 'And that spells trouble.'

'Who are his two friends?'

'Jackson and his sister, Forrest.'

'Is that the famous Forrest-with-two-r's I've heard about at school?' I asked.

'That's her,' laughed Tina. 'Forrest-with-two-r's, in person.'

I stared back over my shoulder at them as they walked off. Charlie's Gang. It was not good news. Charlie Smugg never was.

'Anyhow,' Tina rattled on – she's always full of gossip – 'did you know that someone's been pinching dogs?'

'How do you mean – "pinching"? Is someone pinching dogs, stealing them, or is someone actually pinching them, like pinching their bottoms?'

Tina burst out laughing. 'Trevor! Who on earth would go round pinching dogs' bottoms? Of course I mean stealing. Two dogs have disappeared in the last few days. One was from our street.'

'I know. I saw some posters yesterday. There's a reward of fifty pounds.' I looked at Streaker still trying to pull my arms off and at Mouse, who must weigh as much as an elephant. 'Don't worry. Nobody will want to pinch this pair,' I said flatly.

'Probably not,' agreed Tina, and she chattered on about this and that. That's one thing about Tina: you don't have to say all that much because she's usually too busy talking herself.

When I got home with Streaker Dad was already well under way with wallpapering the back room, which has double doors to the garden. They were wide open to let in some fresh air as Dad busied himself with the wallpapering.

I stood in the doorway with Streaker still on her lead and admired Dad's work and made encouraging noises, such as telling him which bits he'd missed with the paste and so on.

I'd only been there for about a minute when something rather weird happened. A chicken wandered into the room. It was a white cockerel with a big red crown on its head. Before I could say anything Streaker had shot after it. She went zooming after the squawking bird, which flapped furiously, sending a handful of little feathers up into the air, while Streaker skidded across the floor, knocking over Dad's big bucket of paste.

'Oh, for pity's sake!' yelled Dad. He started back down his ladder, but Streaker and the cockerel were now on their third lap of the

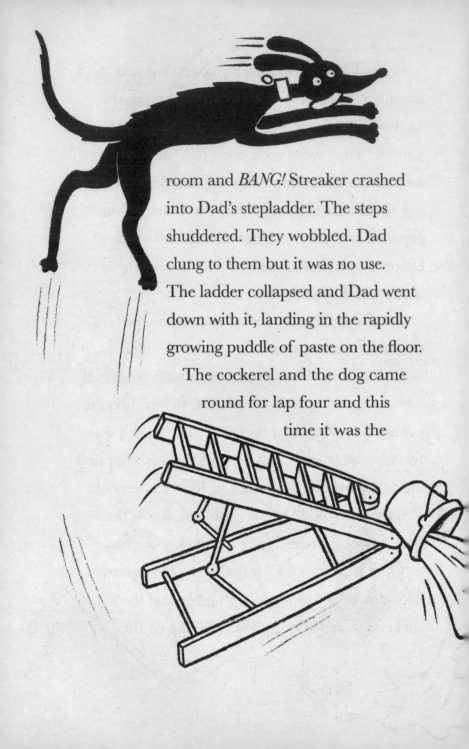

room and *BANG!* Streaker crashed into Dad's stepladder. The steps shuddered. They wobbled. Dad clung to them but it was no use. The ladder collapsed and Dad went down with it, landing in the rapidly growing puddle of paste on the floor.

The cockerel and the dog came round for lap four and this time it was the

pasting table that got involved. Its thin
legs broke and the sheet of ready-pasted
paper slid off and enveloped Dad.
He tried to fight his way out, but the
paper took hold and soon there was a
wallpaper monster charging round the
room after Streaker and the cockerel
– or maybe they were chasing Dad.

Mum came rushing in, threw her hands up in horror, slipped on the paste, crashed into Dad, bounced off him, then rebounded off the half-collapsed pasting table and just happened to fall right in the path of the fleeing cockerel and grabbed it with both hands.

'GOT – *OOOFFF!*' she started, but the words were thumped out of her by first Streaker and then Dad crashing into her. Dad slumped to the floor and stared at the scene of chaos that surrounded him and that was when he decided once and for all. His mouth opened very, very wide and he roared like a dozen volcanoes.

'BOOT CAMP!!!'

4. We Will Find Your Pet

'Dad! It wasn't Streaker's fault. It was that stupid chicken!' I protested.

'And that stupid dog,' seethed Dad, peeling bits of wallpaper from his face. 'Not to mention that weirdy-beardy nutter who lives up the road with his goat and tortoise and all those hens.'

Excuse me? Who was Dad calling a 'weirdy-beardy nutter'? Did he mean my friend Nicholas's dad? Nicky lives two roads away and his dad's got a brilliant mini-farm in the back garden. There's a goat and hens and rabbits and a tortoise.

'It's not Nicky's dad's fault if one of the chickens escapes,' I said. 'And you can't blame Streaker.'

'Of course I can blame Streaker. I AM

blaming Streaker,' growled Dad. 'Streaker won't do anything I say. She is untrained. She's a rogue elephant!'

I thought calling Streaker a rogue elephant was a bit much. Streaker wasn't a bit like any kind of elephant.

'She can't go to boot camp,' I muttered.

Dad lifted his chin (which had a wallpaper beard stuck to it) and fixed me with his SAD stare. Dad's SAD stare didn't mean he was sad. The letters SAD meant that the Shutters Are Down. In other words, Dad had stopped listening. He had made up his mind. He would do whatever it was he'd said he would do and this time he had decided that Streaker was going to go to boot camp and That Was That. Things could not look any worse really. Dad might just as well have sentenced Streaker to a firing squad.

I sighed. Now I had just a few hours to get Streaker out of the house and safely across to Tina's house. This would mean I'd get into trouble, but there was no choice. I was on a mission. I was going to save Streaker's life. Dad would shout at me for a bit, but Streaker would be safe.

I looked at my faithful four-legged companion and my faithful four-legged companion carried on chewing up bits of wallpaper as if they were cheese sandwiches and didn't pay any attention to me or my dad.

In the meantime, I was told to take the cockerel back to the mini-farm round the corner. (Actually, it's round TWO corners.) I left Streaker at home and hoped she wouldn't get into any more trouble while I was away. I tucked the cockerel under one arm and set off.

Nicholas must have spotted me marching up

the path because he opened the door even before I'd had time to knock.

'You found Captain Birdseye!' Nicholas exclaimed, plucking the chicken from beneath my arm.

'Boo!' shouted a small tousled head sticking out between Nicholas's knees. It was his three-year-old brother, Cheese, the one with the famous bottom.

'Boo to you,' I answered, but Cheese had already disappeared back into the house. I filled Nicholas in about all the adventures of Captain Birdseye, not to mention what it meant for Streaker.

'Oh, I'm really sorry.' Nicholas looked pretty glum, but, as he pointed out, it hadn't been the chicken's fault. 'But at least Streaker will be safe from being stolen.'

'Oh? Has another dog gone missing?'

Nicholas shook his head 'It's a cat this time. Mrs Steambull's Siamese. Anyhow, sorry Captain Birdseye has given you a problem.'

I shrugged. 'Streaker was bound to do something awful eventually. It's the way she is. But Dad's going to send her to a doggy boot camp so I'm going to hide her at Tina's.'

'Best of luck with Tina,' Nicholas grinned.

'She's not my girlfriend,' I grunted.

'I never said she was,' smiled Nicholas.

'You looked it.'

'It's just my face,' laughed Nicholas. 'It's always showing things it's not meant to.'

I rolled my eyes in disbelief and set off back home. On the way I got a bit of a surprise because I spotted yet another small poster stuck to a lamp post and another one soon after that. Time for a closer look.

LOST PET?
WE WILL FIND IT FOR YOU!
REASONABLE RATES.
CONTACT
LOST PETS R US
TEL: 072 00123

Hmmm, interesting. I wonder how you go about searching for a lost pet? Follow a trail of paw prints? Sniff them out? Oh well, good luck to them.

As soon as I got home I told Mum that I was going to take Streaker for a walk.

'Don't be long,' she warned. 'Your dad has been on the phone to the boot camp squad and they're coming to fetch Streaker in two hours' time.'

Two hours! I'd have to be quick. I nodded and clipped Streaker's lead on to her collar. I felt like some kind of superhero. OK, so maybe I'm a rather small eleven-year-old superhero whose costume is a pair of torn jeans and a blue T-shirt that has DON'T ASK ME, ASK MY DOG written on the front in big yellow letters. Not much of a costume, eh? But then, I thought, if you are a superhero, isn't it better to be in disguise? You don't want anyone to know you're a superhero because there would be no element of surprise, would there? You'd come zooming up to

a crime scene, a bank robbery say, and everyone
would go – 'Wow! Look, here's SuperTrev! Go,
SuperTrev! Get the bank robbers!'

Then the bank robbers would look at each
other and say, 'Uh-oh, SuperTrev is here. We'd
better make a run for it!' And they'd dash off
with all the money they'd stolen and SuperTrev,
in other words ME, would be too late. No, it was

definitely better to be a superhero in disguise and today I, Trevor, would save Streaker!

By this time I'd arrived at Tina's house. It never takes long to get there because (a) she lives close by and (b) Streaker always pulls me along at speeds that break the sound barrier – three times.

Tina opened the door, saw me and Streaker and raised both eyebrows. 'Has your –'

'Yes,' I interrupted because I wanted to get inside to safety as soon as possible.

'So you're –'

'Exactly,' I agreed. Tina opened the door wider.

'Do you want to –'

'Yes! Of course I want to come in and hide Streaker,' I snapped, hastily looking behind me to make sure that Dad wasn't hard on my heels.

'Well, I'm pleased to see you too,' Tina snapped back sarcastically, but she held the door open and Streaker pulled me inside so fast I tripped on the step and was launched straight into Tina's arms.

'At last!' she sighed with a radiant smile, closing
her arms round me. I struggled free and glared
at her, saved by the appearance of Tina's mother.
I hardly recognized her. She had dyed her
normally mousey-brown hair coal black, with a
wide blonde streak down one side.

'You've had your hair done,' I said, and Tina
burst out laughing.

'Honestly, Trev, a blind whale can see that!'

I reddened. 'I like it,' I said, though I'm not

sure I did. For some reason the new hairstyle made me think of zebras, and badgers, not to mention skunks.

'Thank you, Trevor, what a well-brought-up boy you are, unlike my daughter here,' Tina's mum commented. 'I'm sorry you're having problems with Streaker, and your father. The dog can stay for a few days, but that's the best I can offer.'

I nodded gratefully and followed Tina, Streaker and Mouse upstairs to Tina's room. We sat down and plotted how best to disguise my crazy canine.

'She can't stay indoors all the time,' I said. 'She'll need to go out and – you know.'

'Have a tiddly-widdly wee?' suggested Tina. Then she added, as if it made things any better, 'That's what Mum calls it.'

'Whatever,' I murmured.

'I've embarrassed you,' grinned Tina.

I tried to count the number of times Tina had embarrassed me in the past, but soon gave up because there were so many. Trying to embarrass me was Tina's favourite game and rather annoying. She nudged me playfully.

'You know I only do it to annoy you.'

'You're succeeding,' I growled. 'Try to think of a subject that isn't so annoying. I've got bored with this one. In any case, how are we going to disguise Streaker? It's going to be pretty difficult. I mean, dogs just look like dogs really.'

'Yes, I know,' agreed Tina. 'Strange, isn't it?'

I glanced at her and we burst out laughing. 'You're such an idiot!' I told her.

'That makes two of us.'

Streaker pushed her way between us while Mouse padded up and laid his huge head on my lap and looked at me with pleading eyes, as if she was hoping I'd give him the biggest choccy ice cream ever.

'Do you really like Mum's new hairstyle?' asked Tina. 'Don't you think it's a bit weird?'

'It's, um, startling,' I decided. 'I expect we'll both

get used to it. It's just that when I look at it I get visions of great herds of zebras charging through my mind. It must be all that black and white.'

Tina suddenly grabbed my arm. She swung round and looked at me intently.

'That's it! You're absolutely right! You are so right! Brilliant! That's what we'll do!'

I was completely in the dark. 'What is what we'll do?' I asked.

'To disguise Streaker!' Tina almost shouted at me. 'We'll turn her into a zebra!'

5. A Very Small Zebra

I looked at Tina and wondered if perhaps she'd
gone completely mad, but she was just smiling
and nodding.

'A zebra?' I repeated, and Tina carried on
nodding. 'OK, I get the black-and-white bit but
the rest? Forget it. You can't turn a small dog
into a zebra. What are you planning to do? Put
Streaker on stilts?'

Tina burst out laughing. 'Good idea! No,
seriously, Trevor, think about it. We can use my
mum's hair dye to give Streaker white stripes, like
a zebra.'

'She'd have to be a very small zebra,' I
muttered.

'I never meant she should look like a real
zebra. I just meant we could give her stripes

LIKE a zebra. Nobody will recognize her. Isn't that what you want?'

I had to admit that of course it was. 'It's just a bit peculiar,' I grunted, and I stared at Streaker, who had no idea what we were planning. She'd been busily rooting around under Tina's bed and suddenly reappeared with a pair of knickers dangling over her head.

'Thank YOU!' Tina turned rather red and quickly snatched them away. Streaker looked up at her with her tongue hanging out and a silly grin on her face. 'I hope that when you're a zebra you'll have better manners.'

'I'd better get home,' I muttered.

'What will you tell your mum and dad?'

'I'll say Streaker ran off. She does sometimes,

as you know. Anyhow, thanks for looking after her and for the zebra idea.'

'You're not convinced, are you? It's going to work, Trevor. It'll be fine and then you'll be able to take her out for walks and everything. Come back this afternoon and we'll get to work.'

I nodded and set off. I was turning the corner into my road when I almost bumped into Charlie Smugg – and his gang. They were all hooded up, but I instantly recognized Jackson and his sister, Forrest-with-two-r's. The pair were both tall and thin. Jackson's sister was called Forrest-with-two-r's because, when anyone asked her name, that was what she'd say: 'My name is Forrest, with two r's.'

I don't think Forrest is a good name, no matter how many r's it has, especially this Forrest, who was so tall and thin she would only ever be one tree and that wouldn't make much of a forest. I thought this was very funny, but I didn't tell Forrest-with-two-r's because she's bigger and older and, what's more, her brother Jackson is even bigger and older. Now the pair of them were hanging about with Charlie Smugg.

'Look who it isn't,' sneered Charlie. 'Been to see your itsy-bitsy girlfriend?'

'She's a friend, not a girlfriend,' I said, and glanced at Forrest-with-two-r's. 'What's happened to Sharon? Have you dumped her? Is Forrest-with-two-r's YOUR girlfriend now?'

Charlie stepped dangerously close and I took a step back. 'It's none of your business, little boy,' he spat. 'This is my gang.'

'What does your gang do?' I asked.

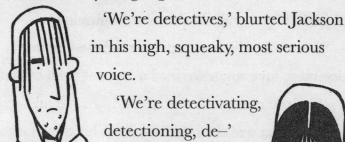

'We're detectives,' blurted Jackson in his high, squeaky, most serious voice.

'We're detectivating, detectioning, de—'
Forrest-with-two-r's gave up trying to say 'detecting' and eventually mumbled, 'We're looking.'

Charlie folded his arms in an effort to look important. 'Yeah, that's right. Someone has been stealing pets and me and my gang are looking for 'em. When we find 'em we'll give 'em back to their owners.'

The penny dropped. The posters on the lamp posts! It was Charlie and his gang.

'You're LOST PETS R US?' I asked in disbelief. I'm surprised Charlie can find his own feet, let alone a missing pet. I guess he wants to be a policeman, like his dad, Sergeant Smugg,

57

who is quite possibly the worst policeman on the planet. (He's certainly the most annoying.)

'Yeah,' Charlie sneered. 'And now we're out detecting and when we find a lost pet we'll take it back to the owner.'

'And what will they do?' I asked.

'Pay us of course,' grinned Charlie.

'We're going to be rich,' smiled Forrest-with-two-r's. 'It's Charlie's idea. He's really clever, is Charlie.' She beamed an even bigger smile at Charlie.

'You ARE his girlfriend!' I declared. 'I feel very sorry for you and you'd better watch out. Sharon's a real tiger. She won't be pleased, will she, Charlie?'

'You shut your trap before I shut it for you,' he hissed.

'Don't worry, I'm off,' I grinned, and I pushed past them and headed for home.

Mum was in the back garden. She was wearing her all-in-one running-swimming-cycling suit and she was practising getting on and off her bike while running. The bike was propped against a tree. Mum was running round the garden and trying to leap on to it.

This was not as easy as it seems because the bike's pedals had special clasps on them for the feet. That meant that Mum had to take a running jump, get her legs either side of the bike frame and push her toes into the pedal clasps ALL AT THE SAME TIME. Which was very DIFFICULT, if not IMPOSSIBLE.

So, in fact, she was spending most of her time falling off the bike and crashing to the ground.

'It's really difficult, Trevor,' Mum complained, as she lay on the grass, wrestling with the bike. 'But I've got to learn how to do it.' She glanced beyond me and frowned. 'Where's Streaker?'

'She ran off. You know what she's like. She'll turn up later.' I spoke casually.

'But your father –' began Mum, then shrugged. 'That will have to wait, but maybe she hasn't run off. You know pets have been disappearing, stolen? And some company or other is offering to track them down.'

'It's not a company, Mum, it's Charlie Smugg and his gang, except they're calling themselves LOST PETS R US.'

'He's got a gang? I don't like the sound of that.'

'Don't worry, Mum, it's only Jackson and his sister.'

'Forrest-with-two-r's?' Mum chuckled. 'I love that name. Well, I see what you mean. I don't think Jackson and Forrest will ever manage to rob the Bank of England. Charlie Smugg might,' she mused, 'but those two – never! They're a bit like lost pets themselves, poor dears. But what about Streaker? Maybe she's been stolen.'

'Mum, she ran off, that's all. She'll be OK. Besides, who would want to steal Streaker? They'd have to be mad.'

Mum smiled. 'You've got a point there. You know, Trevor, I'm sorry your father is going to send her to boot camp, but you do understand, don't you? It's the only way to get her trained. We've tried everything else.'

'Yeah.' I stuck my hands in my pockets and slouched off. A few moments later there was the crash of something falling and a loud yell from Mum. I turned round to look. Mum and her bicycle were collapsed in a tangled heap again.

'Should I call an ambulance?' I offered.

'Don't be cheeky.'

'Do you want a hand getting up?'

'No, Trevor, I don't want a hand getting up, thank you. I have had a lot of practice this morning at getting UP. It's the getting ON I can't manage.'

6. Ta-da! Introducing the Afghan Zebra Hound

I left Mum to it and braced myself for Dad. Much to my surprise he was in a good mood because he had just beaten Sergeant Smugg at golf.

'Streaker will be back soon and then it'll be *PIFFF!*' Dad clapped his hands together and beamed at me.

'*Pifff?*' I repeated. It sounded like a smell to me and I had no idea what Dad was going on about.

'*Pifff!* and Streaker will vanish,' Dad declared. 'She'll be whisked away by the boot camp guards and when she is returned she'll be a different dog, a very different dog.'

Ah! That's what Dad meant by *pifff!* Obviously, it was supposed to be the noise a dog makes

when it disappears. Hmmm. It still seemed to
me to be far more like the unpleasant SMELL
a dog leaves when it's making itself rather
NOTICEABLE!

I smiled to myself.
Little did Dad know
that Streaker was
definitely going to be
a very different dog
and much sooner than
he thought. Streaker was
going to be the smallest zebra
in the universe! So Dad could
go *PIFFF!* as much as he
liked.

Well, at least I'd broken the news to my
parents. Streaker was missing (ha ha! As if!) so
now I could safely go back to Tina's and set
about stage two of our plan.

'Have you seen the LOST PETS R US
posters?' I asked as I left.

'Yes,' said Dad. 'What's that all about?'

'You know pets have been disappearing? Charlie Smugg and his gang are offering to find them. LOST PETS R US is actually Charlie, Jackson and Forrest.'

'With-two-r's?' asked Dad, and I nodded.

'Those three couldn't find their own feet,' Dad murmured in disbelief.

'I know,' I said and I had to grin. Dad and me actually agreed on something for once! We were united and it felt good!

'I'm going to Tina's,' I announced, just as there was a shout from the garden. It was Mum. She'd got tangled up in her bicycle again.

'Have you got a metal saw?' she shouted at Dad. 'I don't think I can escape otherwise . . .'

Definitely time to go and sort Streaker out!

Tina was pleased to see me. 'I need you desperately,' she said. 'Come in, come in.' She reached out and yanked me indoors so I made sure I didn't trip on the doorstep and fall into her arms again. As it turned out she was only worried about Streaker.

'I don't know how you cope with your dog. She's been driving Mum and me round the bend and back again, not to mention up the wall and across the ceiling. Even Mouse has stopped trying to keep up with her. He's lying in the corner with his tongue halfway across the floor. He's in a complete state of collapse.'

'She needs to be outside so she can let off steam,' I explained. 'Once we've turned her into a zebra we can take her out and she'll be fine.'

'Good. Now listen, Trev, I've had a great idea.'

Uh-oh. Tina and her ideas. My heart sank. 'Go on,' I said warily

'You'll love this. I found a whole pile of hair extensions that Mum isn't using any more.'

'Er, what are hair extensions?'

'They're bits of hair. You attach them to your own hair and it makes it look longer.'

I shook my head. 'I'm happy with my hair as it is. I don't want it longer.'

Tina burst out laughing. 'It's not for you, dimbo! It's for Streaker!'

Hmmm, hair extensions on a dog. What would that make her look like? I wasn't sure.

'She'll look like an Afghan hound,' nodded Tina.

'I thought she was going to be a zebra?'

'She is, but now she'll be more like an Afghan zebra.'

'They don't have zebras in Afghanistan. At least I don't think they do.'

Tina grabbed both my shoulders and shook me hard. 'Will you please stop going on about pointless stuff? Just listen to me. You remember that time we tried to wash Streaker in the bath and there was water everywhere and Mum got rather annoyed? We don't want that to happen again. So we dye the hair extensions white and then fix them to Streaker and she'll become a black-and-white Afghan Zebra Hound. She'll be a new special breed.'

Was Tina crazy? I don't know. Maybe I'm crazy too. Anyhow, that is what we did. The first bit was dead easy. We got the hair extensions. We laid them out on strips of foil. We pasted the dye on the extensions, closed up the foil and left them for half an hour. We opened up the foil packets and BINGO! (or should I say *PIFFF!?*) the brown hair had turned white. Perfect.

All we had to do now was attach them to Streaker.

HA HA HA HA HA HA HA HA HA HA HA HA HA HA HA HA HA HA HA HA HA HA!

(That is supposed to be utterly crazy and despairing laughter. Attaching ANYTHING to Streaker is like trying to stick something on a starship covered in soap and flying at Warp Factor Twenty-three and a Half.)

At least we'd managed to shut Tina's bedroom door before we started. Inside the bedroom were Tina, myself, Mouse and Streaker. There was also a bed, a chest of drawers and a wardrobe.

Then we began. I could not believe how quick and slippery that dog was. No sooner had we got

her pinned down than she escaped and was off
again. Streaker was yelping, Mouse was howling,
Tina was shouting and I had my teeth gritted so
hard I thought I would never get them ungritted.
Before long most of the drawers from the chest
had been knocked out or over and Tina's clothes
were merrily flying around the room, along with
Streaker and Mouse, who obviously thought that
they were playing Follow My Leader While We
All Play At Dressing Up In Tina's Clothes.

The wardrobe went over with an almighty crash, spilling even more clothes, plus games and toys and goodness knows what else into the room. The bedcovers had become caught up in Mouse's back legs so they were also being dragged every

which way. The noise was horrendous – shouts, howls, yelps, barks, curses, screams, not to mention the bangs and thuds and crashes as Tina's bedroom was hit by Typhoon Streaker and Tornado Mouse.

Of course Tina's mum thought
the house was falling down and
came dashing upstairs. The door
opened. Or rather Tina's mum
started to open the door and
then it was smashed back

against the wall as Streaker and Mouse
burst from the bedroom, trailing
bedcovers and blouses, shoes and shorts,
knickers, knick-knacks and nightdresses.
Off they went, careering around
the house.

It took ten minutes to calm them both down. Then the questioning started.

'What is Streaker doing looking like – like – THAT? Why is Mouse wearing a dress? Are those my hair extensions? Is that my hair dye? What's going on? Do I live in a madhouse or is it a zoo? Don't either of you have any sense of responsibility? You've probably scared those two dogs half to death. Whose idea was this?'

And so on, until Tina's mum finished with: 'I want that dog out of the house RIGHT NOW!'

Did she mean Streaker? She certainly did.

Oh dear. Problems. I was going to have to take Streaker

back home. Where else could I take her? Except there was one ray of hope: Streaker didn't look like Streaker any more. She was an Afghan Zebra Hound with black-and-white stripes. Mum and Dad would be very confused. There was no telling what they'd say or do.

I put Streaker on her lead and headed towards home as slowly as I could manage, considering I was being pulled by a four-legged rocket. I needed time to think. I stopped by a wall so I could sit down for a moment and work out what to do.

I don't know how Streaker did it, but she slipped her lead. I didn't even notice her go, but go she did and then she was gone. *Pifff!* as Dad might say. I couldn't blame her. She was probably still traumatized by what had happened in Tina's bedroom. She'd probably gone off to find a doggy psychiatrist.

I was on my feet in an instant, racing up the road. You might ask why I didn't race *down* the road? I don't know. I had no idea which direction Streaker had taken. I just panicked because I was desperate to find her and so off I went, running as fast as I could. I reached the end of the road, rounded the corner and crashed straight into Charlie and his gang of two. Jackson almost dropped the big heavy bag he was carrying.

'Hey, watch it, fish-face!' Charlie scowled, and he grabbed me, but I didn't let him get any further.

'Have you seen Streaker?' I was pretty frantic and Charlie quickly put me down.

'Streaker?' he repeated, as if his brain had just died and he was a jellyfish with no idea who or what I was talking about.

'Yes, Streaker – or for that matter any dog,' I panted desperately, remembering that Streaker now looked like goodness-knows-what. 'Have you seen any dogs come past?'

The three gangsters looked at each other in a weird way as if they'd just landed from another planet and didn't understand anything.

'Us?' Charlie shook his head and the other two shrugged. 'Why would we have seen any dogs? Just watch where you're going, fish-face.'

They hurried off. Forrest-with-two-r's looked anxiously back at me for a moment and then they'd gone, clutching their bag. I gazed after them. What a weird crew. But I had more important things on my mind, namely one lost dog.

I trailed home with no dog and no hope. Tina and I had probably scared Streaker into the most awful state. What on earth was I to do now? And where was Streaker? There was a dog-napper on the loose and Streaker was out there on her own. I squeezed my eyes tight. I couldn't bear to think of what might happen.

7. Problems – Again!

Now what? If it wasn't one thing it was another.
I had hardly got back home when the guys from
the doggy boot camp arrived at the door. There
were two of them and they looked like the most
evil pair on the planet. For a start they wore
bright Day-Glo orange uniforms, shiny black
rubber gloves and heavy black boots.

They were big too. In fact, the biggest one,
Dimitri, looked like some gargantuan wrestler
about to burst out of his uniform. He even
had huge bulging muscles in his ears, and his
eyebrows were massive, like a pair of giant sea
slugs about to suddenly leap from his face and
suck out all your blood.

His pal was called Grunt or maybe it was
meant to be Grant. The way Dimitri spoke it

sounded like Grunt and it suited him. Grunt was the closest thing to a real Neanderthal caveman I had ever seen. He was even hairier than Dimitri and he was all muscle too, but shorter than his pal. The oddest thing about him was his head. It was tiny! There was this big muscle-pumping body with almost no neck and then a tiny head perched on top, like a pebble on a mountain peak. His eyes were so close together they almost touched.

'Dog!' grunted Grunt.

Dad took a step back. He looked pretty scared of this pair too. 'Ah,' began Dad. 'Well, you see –'

'Dog!' Grunt grunted more loudly.

'She ran away,' Dad explained.

'DOG!'

'Oh dear,' Dad muttered to himself and scratched his head. 'Dog gone. Ran away.' He put his arms up like two paws, stuck out his tongue and made a panting noise. 'Dog – *whoosh!* Gone!'

I thought, *Wow! That's a pretty good dog impression, Dad!*

Grunt looked at Dimitri. His face wore a hideous frown, as if it was about to collapse in on itself like some black hole. Dimitri put a calming hand on Grunt's shoulder.

'You mean the dog isn't here?' Dimitri asked, and Dad relaxed and put down his paws. Hooray! One of them did understand after all.

'Exactly. She ran away a couple of hours ago and we haven't seen her since. Searched everywhere but there's no sign.'

Dimitri nodded. 'Looks like a case of a runaway dog.'

'Yes,' agreed Dad.

Dimitri pulled out his mobile and began punching in numbers. He glanced at my father. 'Runaway dogs must be reported to the police. Can't have a runaway dog. It might attack someone.'

Dad groaned. 'Is that really necessary? Streaker is quite harmless.'

'I thought you said she was untrainable,' Dimitri shot back. 'Isn't that why you called us in?'

'Well, yes, but –'

'An untrained dog on the loose puts innocent children at risk,' Dimitri began before breaking off to speak on his mobile. 'Ah, Sergeant Smugg? Bit of a problem. Dog on the loose. Yes, ran off. Gone wild. Colour? Black-ish. Name? Streaker.'

Dimitri held the phone away from his ear as Sergeant Smugg shouted back down the phone at him. Even Dad and I could hear what the policeman was saying.

'Streaker! That dog is a terrorist! I'm sick to death of hearing about that dog. She should be deported and sent back to her own country! She's a criminal. I've lost count of the number of times I've arrested that creature, but somehow she always manages to get away, pretending she's so innocent. Well, I'm going to get her this time. If you catch her you bring her straight to me and I'll deal with her properly once and for all.'

There was a loud click as Sergeant Smugg slammed the phone down at his end. Dimitri slipped his mobile into his pocket and turned to my dad.

'Seems like your dog is a bit of a problem, sir. OK, Grunt, you'd better keep the catching nets and the stun gun close by, just in case. Let's get back to the van and we'll cruise around for a bit and see if we can catch this rogue hound.'

They left and Dad and I went into the front room. I looked at my father. It was a special look, one that spoke silent words, and my silent words said – *Now look what's happened and this is all because*

you wanted Streaker to go to boot camp, just because she
played in the sand at your precious golf club and she
chased a chicken. Now Sergeant Smugg wants to get his
hands on her and you know how much he hates Streaker –
and us.

Dad wilted. His face turned white and pasty. 'Don't look at me like that, Trevor. I'm sorry but it's not my fault.'

'It's as much your fault as Streaker's,' I pointed out.

'She was with you when she ran away,' Dad shot back. We were like two gunslingers facing each other for a showdown on a dusty street, except we were in the front room by the telly and the only thing Dad was armed with was his car keys and I only had a used tissue in my pocket. Maybe I could attack him with snot . . .

In the end, we both backed down. After all, the important thing was to find Streaker and get her back safe and sound. Trouble was, now the Doggy Squad from the boot camp AND the police were also hunting for her.

There was of course one thing in Streaker's favour and I wasn't sure whether or not I should tell Dad quite yet. Streaker was in disguise. However, the disguise Tina and I had chosen did make Streaker rather noticeable. It's not every day you might see an Afghan Zebra Hound come racing past you with a stolen burger in its mouth. (Streaker is very good at stealing burgers – and pies, chips, pizzas, ice creams and so on.)

The problem was that if I told Dad about the disguise I would also have to admit that I'd lied about Streaker running away. Uh-oh. What should I do? It was bad enough that Streaker had run off like that, but now she was at the mercy of a gang of dognappers AND she was being hunted down by the Boot Camp Bunch

AND Sergeant Smugg and the police. It really couldn't get much worse. In the end, I asked myself: what's the most important thing in all this horrible mess I'd got myself into? And the answer was STREAKER. So I had to be brave – and honest.

I found Dad in the back garden. He was trying to rescue Mum from her bicycle again and was suggesting that maybe she should leave out the cycling bit of the triathlon.

'Just do the swimming and running,' he told her.

'Don't be daft,' laughed Mum. 'It's a triathlon. That means it's got three bits to it. You can't leave out one of them. That would be like doing the pole vault without a pole. Oh dear, Trevor's here and he's got a very long face as if he's carrying half the world on his shoulders. This must be something serious.'

I don't know how my parents do it. They always seem to know when there's something on my mind, especially Mum. She takes one look at me and says: 'What's wrong?' or 'What's bothering you then?'

Mum beckoned me over. 'Come on, spit it out. What's wrong? Is it Streaker?'

Well, of course it was Streaker. It was nearly always Streaker. So I opened my mouth and downloaded the story of Streaker and Tina and how the family dog was now an Afghan Zebra Hound.

Do you know what? Do you know what my parents did? They burst out laughing! In fact, they couldn't stop.

'Stop it!' I shouted. 'Stop laughing! Streaker's in danger!'

'But Trevor,' cried Mum, 'Streaker dressed as an Afghan Zebra Hound! I can't wait to see. Does Tina's mother know what's happened to her hair extensions? No, of course she doesn't. What a stupid question. Oh, Trevor! I do hope you never grow up.'

What? What was she on about now? I shall never understand my parents. I was standing there, watching them laugh their heads off, while Streaker was probably running for her life and in the greatest danger ever.

Then Dad's mobile rang. In an instant, there was silence – apart from the phone. Mum and I looked at Dad. He looked at us. Who could it be? Sergeant Smugg? The Dog Squad? Was it bad news? Had they found Streaker?

Dad reached into his pocket and carefully pulled out his phone as if it was a small bomb. He put it to his ear and a moment later I noticed his body relax. It wasn't bad news then.

'Really?' Dad spoke into the phone. 'When? OK. Of course.' He switched off his mobile.

'Who was that?' Mum and I were both puzzled.

'That was Ron. You know, the beardy-weirdy, Nicholas's father. I rang him earlier because I was so annoyed about his escaped chicken and I wanted to complain. He's just rung me to say that someone has stolen his goat.'

'His goat? Rubbish?'

'No, it's not rubbish, it's true,' argued Dad.

'No, Dad, I know it's true. I didn't mean it was a rubbish story. Their goat is called Rubbish.'

'The goat's called Rubbish? What kind of name is that for a goat?' Dad paused for a moment and smiled. 'It's a rubbish name, that's what!'

'And that's a rubbish joke, Dad,' I added for good measure.

BUT – what was going on? Why would anyone

steal A GOAT? And, if they could steal a goat, why not steal an Afghan Zebra Hound? My heart clenched into a fist. If anything happened to Streaker I, I – I simply couldn't bear to even think about it.

8. Aha! Sherlock Holmes Cracks the Case!

I think I'm turning into Sherlock Holmes. Animals are going missing all over the place. Why? Who was taking them? Even Mum and Dad were getting concerned.

'I hope Streaker's all right,' Dad muttered.

I was so surprised I thought it was a joke and almost burst out laughing. I was about to say, *But Dad, you hate Streaker*, when I saw his face and he really, really meant it. I shall never understand my parents.

Anyhow, Mum was about to depart for her big triathlon. Apparently, there were going to be lots of competitors, about two hundred, Mum reckoned.

'I just hope I don't come last,' she said.

'There's no way you'll be last, Mum,' I said.
'You're amazing! And you know what they say –
run like the wind, swim like a fish and pedal like
– um –'

'An idiot with feet like a penguin?' suggested
Mum.

'No! Pedal like crazy!'

'I must be crazy to be taking part,' said Mum.

'You'll be fine,' Dad told her. 'I'll wait for you
up at the finishing line. How about you, Trevor?'

I nodded. 'I'll be there, but I have to go and
see Tina first and work out what we can do about
Streaker. I've got to find her.'

'I know, I know,' murmured Dad and HE
RUFFLED MY HAIR! I hastily tried to smooth
it back down, but I set off for Tina's wearing a
big grin.

Tina's mother didn't seem all that pleased to
see me. I can't imagine why.

'What are you planning to do this time,
Trevor? Want some hair extensions for yourself

maybe? Or perhaps you'd like to cover Mouse in my make-up?'

I gave her a weak smile as if I thought she was funny. (As if!) 'Sorry about last time.'

Tina's mum shook her head and beckoned me inside. 'She's upstairs, cleaning the bathroom. God help the world if you two ever get married.'

'We're just friends.' How many billion times did I have to repeat myself?

Tina's mum snorted. 'Huh. That's what Cleopatra said when she was with Mark Antony and look what happened to them.'

I had no idea what had happened to Cleopatra and Mark Antony, but I did know that she was Queen of Ancient Egypt and he was a Roman bigwig. Tina's mum noticed my blank face and explained.

'They fell for each other, Trevor, big time. Their love affair started a war with Rome and they lost. Mark Antony killed himself and when Cleopatra heard about it she famously committed

suicide by allowing a small but deadly poisonous snake to bite her. Let that be a lesson to you, Trevor.'

'Like I said, we're friends. Marriage is not on the menu.'

I went upstairs. Tina was in the bathroom, just as her mother had said. She was in as bad a mood as her mother, so now all three of us felt grumpy.

'Look who's turned up,' growled Tina. 'Just in time to be of no help at all as I've just finished cleaning everything.'

'I didn't know you'd even started. I would've helped if I'd been here.'

'Sure. So what's new?'

'Your mum thinks I'm Mark Antony and you're Cleopatra and you're going to get bitten by a snake and die.'

Tina put down the sponge she'd been using. 'That's nice of her. It makes you feel really good to know that your own mother thinks things like that about you.'

I shook my head. 'I know. Apparently, Mark Antony kills himself too. Stupid, if you ask me. Why didn't they just run away and live in a cave or something?'

'Exactly.' Tina nodded. 'And another thing: what is the point of having two names? I mean you're either Mark or you're Antony. It's stupid to be called both. It's like calling yourself Trevor James or Louis Wayne.'

'Or Tina Selina,' I suggested.

'Exactly,' Tina said. She was a bit more

cheerful now that she'd done a bit of complaining. 'Anyhow, why are you here, Mark Antony?'

'I have come to seek your advice, O Great Queen of the Desert.'

'Queen of the Dessert? What kind of dessert would that be, Mark Antony? Would it be ice cream?'

'No, O Mighty Queen, for I did not say "dessert", I said desert, you deaf crazy person.'

'How dare you insult the Queen of Dessert! Take that! And that!' Tina threw her sponge at me, closely followed by a tube of toothpaste.

'OK, I give in,' I announced. 'I shall now stab myself with this sponge and so – I die! Urgh!' I collapsed to the floor in my death throes.

BIG MISTAKE!!!

Tina rushed over to me, lifted my head and cradled it in her arms. 'O Mark, or is it Antony? Do not die! Do not leave me! O Mark! O Antony! (How many people are you?!) One last kiss, that's

all I ask. One last kiss! Or maybe two – one from Mark and one from Antony.'

'NOOOOO!' I yelled, jumping to my feet as fast as I could. Phew. Was that a narrow escape or what?

It was definitely time to get down to the business in hand. Being Sherlock Holmes would be a lot safer than being Mark Antony. I told Tina about the stolen goat and what had happened when I got home.

'Animals are disappearing all over the place,' I finished. 'Something weird is going on and I'm sure Streaker has got herself involved somehow.

Somebody must be taking them but why?'

'I know, and guess what? My aunt's poodle has been stolen. She had one of those leaflets pushed through the letterbox.'

'What leaflets?'

'The ones that Charlie Smugg, pet detective, posts. Didn't you get one?'

'Don't think so, although Mum and Dad might have picked it up and not shown me. There are lots of things they don't show me. My parents are very secretive. I think maybe they're working for a foreign spy network and I'm only their son as some kind of camouflage to stop the neighbours realizing that they're living slap-bang next door to a dangerous pair of international terrorists.'

'Have you finished?' Tina demanded.

'Stranger things have happened,' I hinted, waggling my eyebrows at her.

DON'T
ASK ME,
ASK
MY
DOG

'Only in your head, Trevor. Now stop fantasizing and sending me secret messages in eyebrow code. Back to those leaflets.'

'Did you and your mum get one?' I asked.

'No, but my aunt did. I just told you.'

'The one with the poodle?' My brain was going into overdrive, which is always a very exciting moment. 'Give me your mobile,' I said.

'Why?'

'Because I need it. Come on, quick! This is important. Thanks. Now Nicholas's number. Yep. Shh! It's ringing.'

Nicholas answered the phone himself. I asked a couple of questions, thanked him and handed the phone back to Tina. Did Sherlock Holmes grin madly? Probably. I certainly was. Tina seemed to find it frightening.

'Don't look at me in that scary way,' she said. 'Tell me what he said.'

'OK, listen. Your aunt had her dog stolen. She gets a leaflet from Charlie Smugg offering to find it for her. Rubbish the goat is stolen and guess what? Nicholas says they got a leaflet from Charlie Smugg offering to find it for them. You haven't had a pet stolen and don't get a leaflet so that must mean that –'

'Charlie Smugg is stealing pets and offering to find them AND he's getting paid for it!' yelled Tina. 'It's a scam! It's a great big whopping humungous scam, and you've just worked it out because you're my utterly brilliant and brainy boyfriend!'

LOST PET?
WE WILL FIND IT FOR YOU!
REASONABLE RATES.
CONTACT
LOST PETS R US
TEL: 072 00123

'Friend,' I reminded her but it was no good.

'Boyfriend!' shouted Tina and before I could do anything she'd flung her arms round me and kissed me.

ON THE CHEEK! ON THE CHEEK! JUST ON THE CHEEK! HONEST!

'Put me down and listen,' I protested, pushing Tina away. 'We have to prove it. We can't simply go to Charlie and point the finger at him. We need proof. We have to find where he and his gang are keeping all the pets and maybe catch him at his little game. Plus, we have to find Streaker. She's often run off, but she always comes back after an hour or two. She's never been lost for this long. To tell you the truth, I'm worried sick.'

'Maybe Charlie has *her*,' Tina suggested quietly.

Sometimes Tina can be really annoying, like a few moments ago, and sometimes she can be totally amazing, like she was now. Of course. Charlie may well have stolen Streaker, and because she was disguised as an Afghan Zebra Hound he wouldn't have any idea who she belonged to. And then I suddenly remembered. When Streaker had run away I'd gone after her and crashed into Charlie and what was Jackson holding? A big bag. A heavy bag. Was

Streaker inside? Had they just stolen an Afghan Zebra Hound, not realizing it was my dog? It was certainly more than likely. Tina was right! I almost wanted to give her a thank-you hug. (Almost but not enough to actually do it!)

'You're right. And you're quite brilliant too. Just don't expect a kiss. Come on, it's time to go a-hunting!'

A few minutes later we were out on the street. I thought it would be a good idea to go and see one or two other people who'd lost a pet and find out if they'd got leaflets from Charlie. That would strengthen our case. I also wanted to keep a sharp eye out for any places that Charlie might use to hide the pets. After all, animals can be pretty noisy, especially dogs.

We'd hardly got to the end of Tina's road when we saw Sharon Blenkinsop, Charlie's girlfriend. Or should I say ex-girlfriend? I wasn't sure if Charlie really had hooked up with Forrest-with-two-r's or not. I soon found out.

As soon as Sharon spotted Tina and me she crossed the road and made a beeline for us.

'Have you seen Charlie?' she demanded rather angrily.

'No,' I answered.

'Well, if you do you can tell him from me that he's a piece of lowlife and I hope all those animals of his eat him alive and that Forrest girl too. Stupid name for a girl, if you ask me. The only tree-like thing about her is that she's got a brain made of wood.'

Was that a bit of a giveaway? It certainly was.

'We'll pass the message on,' I said cheerfully. 'He's running a clever scam, isn't he?'

'Yeah. Thinks he can get away with it too,' muttered Sharon. 'He must have at least six up there, including the weirdest dog you've ever seen.'

'What's weird about it?' I asked.

'It's got white stripes. Looks like a doggy zebra, only as if someone's shrunk it.'

'Really?' I tried not to sound too interested. 'Where does Charlie keep all these creatures?'

'Up –' Sharon stopped and looked at me suspiciously. 'Got to go,' she snapped, and hurried off.

I looked at Tina and grinned. 'Did you hear that? "Up" she said. And I think I know exactly where "up" is. Come on!'

9. How to Play Crazy Golf!

Over on the golf course there's an old hut. I
think it used to be for the greenkeepers to store
their equipment in, but they hadn't done that
for a long time. Sometimes kids use it as a kind
of camp and once – ha ha! – Tina and I caught
Charlie Smugg and Sharon snogging there.

I know, it's disgusting, isn't it? Imagine
snogging Charlie Smugg. Or Sharon. Or anyone
for that matter. It'd be like kissing slugs. Not to be
recommended.

Anyhow, we never go up there when the golfers
are about. It's too risky. If they see you then
you're in dead trouble and even if they don't
you might get clobbered by someone's golf ball
whizzing through the air. Some of those golfers
are completely useless and you never know which

direction their ball will go in when they hit it.

Not to mention the flying clubs. I've seen more than one golfer take an almighty swipe

at the ball, miss it completely, let go of the golf club and instead of the ball slicing through the air the club goes helicoptering off – *whang-whang-whang-whang!* Can you imagine how

dangerous that is? Sometimes there's a queue of ambulances waiting to take injured players off to the hospital with golf clubs twisted round their necks. (Ha ha! Just joking!)

Nevertheless, Tina and I had to get up to the hut to discover if we were right about where

Charlie was hiding the stolen pets. Only problem was the golf course was swarming with golfers and golf clubs, and balls were whizzing about

every which way. It was like a war zone.

Tina and I had to wriggle through the long grass to get to the hut. Tina almost screamed when a golf ball plopped down just two metres from her head before rolling towards her. I

thought it would trundle straight into her gawping mouth, but she quickly reverse-wriggled backwards and ran me over.

'Trevor!' she hissed, as if it was my fault.

'Tina!' I hissed back, because it was hers. 'You sat on my head!'

'Shh! Someone's coming!' Tina flattened herself against the ground. Unfortunately, half of her was still on top of me so now my face was pressed firmly into the dirt and I was trying not to eat a mouthful of mud and grass.

'Blurrrrgh!' was the only thing I was able to say.

'Shh!' Tina repeated, as a large hairy hand reached towards us, snatched up the golf ball and then moved away.

I would have breathed a huge sigh of relief if Tina hadn't been crushing me into the ground. All I could do was just try to keep breathing and stay alive.

It was ages before Tina decided it was safe to move again and she rolled off me.

'Thank you,' I said icily, picking bits of grass and earth out of my mouth.

'You always make such a fuss, Trevor. Just enjoy the adventure.'

I opened my mouth to say something, but decided not to. Instead, I raised my head a fraction and peered over the grass to see if the route to the hut was clear.

'They've gone but keep your head down. Get ready to scoot. One, two, three, let's go!'

We bent double and raced across the green to the hut. It was now or never.

'I'm going to open the door a tiny bit, so we can see inside. If the animals are in there we'd best leave them be. Then we can hide and catch Charlie up to his tricks when he comes back.'

'OK,' nodded Tina. 'Let's take a look.'

Well, OK, that was THE PLAN.

Sometimes plans don't work. Or they go wrong. Or the unexpected happens. Or, as in this case, all three happen at the same time. The plan didn't work, it did go wrong AND the unexpected happened. The 'unexpected' came in the shape of a goat called Rubbish. Rubbish was a very lively beast and no doubt she was rather fed up with being shut in the old hut, especially as she had four dogs and three cats for company.

The moment I opened the hut door a tiny crack Rubbish charged at it full tilt.

KERDUMP! KERDUMP! KERDUMP! KERDUMP! (That's the goat charging across the hut bit.)

KERRASH! SMASSHHH! KAPOWW! (That's the kerrash, smasshhh, kapoww bit.)

The door was practically ripped from its hinges and Rubbish came thundering out at top speed, closely followed by four madly barking dogs and

three hysterically howling cats. (And of course one of the dogs was . . . guess who? Streaker! Streaker the Afghan Zebra Hound!)

Tina and I were both thrown to the ground and by the time we got up the eight beasts were zooming towards the nearest group of useless golfers. One was just in mid-swing when she noticed a goat galloping straight at her. She was so surprised she let go of her club and off it went, whirling through the air. A moment later Rubbish mowed her down and headed straight for her companions.

Yells and screams filled the air as the dogs now piled into the scrum, yapping and barking, while the other four golfers ran in four different directions, hotly pursued by Rubbish, the cats and the dogs.

It just so happened that the four golfers were Chief Constable Boffington-Orr, Sergeant Smugg, the golf club manager and my father.

'Arrest those animals!' bellowed the Chief Constable.

'Arrest those children!' yelled Sergeant Smugg.

'It's not our fault,' I began. 'It was –'

'Don't think you can pull the wool over my eyes this time,' Sergeant Smugg interrupted, still at top volume. 'I'm sick to death of all of you.' He turned to my father, red-faced and almost breathless with anger. 'Your children are a menace. They're out of control and always have been!'

'They're not my children!' my dad yelled back.

What! Was Dad saying he wasn't my dad? I wasn't his child? So whose was I?

'Only one of them is my child!' shouted Dad.

Oh, so he *was* my dad after all. I wasn't sure if I was disappointed or relieved. Relieved, I think. Sort of.

'The girl is someone else's,' Dad explained, though it didn't matter since Sergeant Smugg wasn't interested in who our parents were. He was convinced we were first-class criminals.

'Those kids and their dogs! They should all be in jail! I'm arresting the whole lot of you and that includes the goat!' He pulled out his radio. 'Calling all units. All units to the golf course to apprehend and arrest eleven dangerous terrorists, that is to say a boy, a girl, a goat, four dogs, three cats and the children's father! What? Yes! I did say a goat!'

'I'm not the girl's father!' my dad repeated, but again nobody was listening. This was mostly because the dogs were now leaping at all of us and getting very overexcited.

Tina and I didn't mind because we knew

they were
being friendly,
especially Streaker, but the
two policemen and even my dad
thought they were now being attacked
and kept trying to push them away.
That made the dogs jump up

even more because they thought it was such a good game. (Don't ask me what the cats were doing. They had long since disappeared.)

Distant sirens became louder and louder and the next thing was a fleet of police squad cars came driving straight over the golf greens and headed towards us. At the same moment about

two hundred cyclists came racing across from
the other end of the golf course, like a mad herd
of migrating buffalo, puffing and panting and
pedalling like crazy. Before anyone could say
'Oops!' they were all over the place, crashing

into police cars, knocking people over and all the
while trying to avoid the goat and all the dogs.
One cyclist even managed to end up on the roof
of a police car. He simply stood astride his
bike, scratching his head.

It was the golf club manager's turn to go mad. He began screaming and jumping up and down and waving his arms as if he expected to take off at any moment.

'STOP! STOP! You're ruining the course. My lovely greens! They're being churned to bits by your stupid cars! STOP!'

Sergeant Smugg suddenly caught sight of my mother among the cyclists. 'And you can arrest her as well!' he yelled. 'She started it! It's all her fault!'

And with that four police officers pounced on Mum and handcuffed her to the bike and to themselves.

Oh well, what can you do? Not a lot! Tina and I sat down on the grass and watched as one by one the animals were arrested. Rubbish was handcuffed to a young constable and she promptly ate her hat. Tina and I were handcuffed to each other, much to Tina's amusement (but not mine!), and so was my dad (handcuffed, that is to say). We were bundled into a police van and off we went to police headquarters like a bunch of common criminals, while Sergeant Smugg sat next to the van driver and kept saying scary things like, 'Nabbed 'em. Got 'em bang to rights. Fifty years in the clink for this. I'll see 'em all behind bars at last!'

In the darkness at the back of the van, Tina gave me a wan smile and whispered in my ear, 'You can hold my hand if you want.'

Now that REALLY scared me!

10. Arrested – Again!

Streaker was SO pleased to see me. In fact, she
washed my face at least ten times. The other
dogs were happy to be free too and they went
bouncing round, jumping on each of us in turn.
The rear of the van was smelly and jam-packed.

There was Rubbish and all the dogs and cats plus Dad and Tina and me and Mum and Mum's bike and the four police officers who'd managed to handcuff themselves to Mum, or the bike, or another police officer.

One of the police officers fished about in her trouser pocket with her one free hand and produced a small packet. 'Anyone like a –?' she asked, but Streaker snaffled the packet before she could even say 'mint'. The police officer looked at Streaker. 'I guess that was a "yes",' she muttered.

The dogs made Tina and me laugh, but Dad just sat there and told them to get off him and leave him alone.

'They'll never allow me to play at the golf club again,' he sulked. 'And it's all that pesky Streaker's fault. The moment we get home – IF we ever get home and aren't thrown straight into jail, that is – your dog is going straight to boot camp.'

'It wasn't Streaker's fault, Dad. She was stolen by Charlie Smugg. If it's anyone's fault it's his.'

'Huh. Try telling Sergeant Smugg that. He always sticks up for his son. In any case, it wasn't Charlie tearing around the golf course, was it? It was Streaker and her criminal pals. I was so embarrassed.'

Tina flashed a big smile at my father. 'But surely it won't be too bad if you are thrown out of the golf club? You could try tennis instead or bowls. Bowls is a great game for people your age and, after all, you're not really very good at golf, are you?'

Funnily enough, Tina's suggestion didn't brighten my father's day at all. In fact, he quickly went from red, to purple to white with rage and started spluttering and almost foaming at the mouth like some mad creature that should be put down.

'Bowls! People my age! I'm only forty-three! *Bowls!* And what do you mean I'm not very good at golf? How do you know what being good at golf is? You're a girl, almost a baby still!'

I sat back and decided to watch this battle of the Titans. Tina was quick to answer.

'A baby! A girl! I'm eleven years old, not eleven months! And I know as much about golf as you do. I've seen golfers on television. It doesn't take them twenty-three shots to get the ball into one hole. They don't have to fish their ball out of a pond every five minutes and they certainly don't fling their golf clubs through the air at high speed.'

Dad jumped to his feet, at least he tried to jump to his feet, but we were in the police van and he simply banged his head hard against the roof and quickly sat down again.

'Ow! I have never, ever flung my golf clubs through the air!' he yelled.

'Well, your friends certainly have,' Tina declared, arms folded.

'And it wasn't twenty-three shots, it was only twenty-two!'

Tina burst out laughing. 'Twenty-two! Only twenty-two? Well done. You should be a champion in a hundred years' time!'

Dad began spluttering again and turned to me. 'Trevor! Trevor! Don't you ever, ever, EVER marry that girl!'

'We're just good friends, Dad,' I sighed. How many times? A trillion squillion?

By this time the van had reached the police station and screeched to a halt. (Police cars and vans always screech to a halt. I don't know why they can't slow down like normal cars do.)

The van doors were opened and the dogs leaped to freedom. Well, they tried. Unfortunately, they leaped straight into nets being held out by a bunch of dog wardens. As

for Rubbish the goat she was bundled into a large cage. Then we were all marched into the police station and Sergeant Smugg went and stood behind the desk and made himself look terribly important while the chief constable disappeared into his office.

'Right, let's see what we have here. One adult male, aged approximately fifty-five –'

'I'm forty-three!' Dad snarled.

'One adult male who should know better,' the sergeant continued. One boy, male –'

'Of course the boy's male!' interrupted Dad. 'He wouldn't be a boy if he wasn't male, would he?'

Sergeant Smugg ignored my father and went on. 'One girl, female –'

'Aaaargh!' Dad growled through gritted teeth.

'One adult woman, female, and one bicycle,' observed the sergeant.

'Would that be a male or female bicycle, sir?' asked one of the police officers.

'Female,' snapped the sergeant. 'Now then,

what else? One goat, er, female? Male? Just put one goat.' Sergeant Smugg carried on with his list. 'Four dogs, one poodle, one mongrel, one collie and one Afghan Zebra Hound, names unknown.'

'The Afghan Zebra Hound is Streaker,' I told the sergeant.

'Don't be ridiculous. Afghan Zebra Hounds are a very, very special breed of dog and we all know that Streaker is an everyday, very ordinary mongrel. So,' he went on, 'we have here one very valuable rare breed of dog.'

Tina pushed forward, dragging me with her since we were still handcuffed together. 'Trevor's right, it's Streaker,' she said.

Sergeant Smugg began to laugh. 'Come on now. I know an Afghan Zebra Hound when I see one and I also know they're worth a lot of money. Streaker is a mutt, spelled M-U-T!'

'Mutt has two t's at the end,' my father explained.

'Oh, so now a common criminal is going to teach me how to spell?' queried Sergeant Smugg.

'No. I'm just telling you mutt has two t's. It's up to you how you spell it, but if you spell it with one you're going to be wrong. That's all.'

'Whatever.' The policeman shrugged. 'It doesn't change the fact that this dog is not Streaker because she is – perfectly obviously to anyone with eyes as all you have to do is look at her – NOT a mutt with one or two t's: she is an Afghan Zebra Hound.'

'No, she isn't,' contradicted Tina quietly. 'Look.' One by one she started pulling off the white hair extensions. Right before the policeman's eyes the Zebra Hound was becoming less and less zebra and more and more Streaker.

'Stop!' bellowed Sergeant Smugg. 'You'll kill the poor creature. You can't do that! You're ruining her. That's criminal damage to a dog, that is! I'll have you arrested for that!'

'You've already arrested us,' Tina pointed

out. 'Besides, these are hair extensions that I'm
pulling off. And I know they can be pulled off
because Trevor and I put them on her in the first
place.'

'YOU WHAT?! You deliberately disguised a
dog as an Afghan Zebra Hound? That's fraud,
that is. It's against the law! I could arrest you
for that!'

But Tina ignored him and now both she and I were pulling off the extensions until Streaker had become plain old Streaker again.

'There, you see? It's Streaker.' I took a step back so everyone could see.

Sergeant Smugg clapped a hand to his head and sent his cap flying across the room. 'I don't believe it,' he whispered. 'But how? Why?'

I was just about to explain when the door to the police station burst open and in came a very angry, very red-faced Sharon Blenkinsop. She completely ignored Dad and me and Streaker, went striding across to the desk and banged a fist on it.

'That Charlie of yours –' she began.

Sergeant Smugg held up his hand. 'Excuse me, Sharon, but I'm dealing with a very important case of dog forgery.'

'I don't care if there's a dog eating your head! Do you know what I've just seen your Charlie doing? Snogging Forrest-with-two-r's! In the

street! Snogging! Well, that's it. I've had enough
of his two-timing. When you see him you can tell
him it's over with me. I'm dumping him. He's a
two-timing squirrel!'

We all looked at Sharon and chorused,
'Squirrel?'

'You mean "rat",' said Tina. 'Two-timing rat.'

'Same thing,' snapped Sharon. 'And you can
also tell him I'm not interested in Afghan Zebra
Hounds, no matter how valuable they are.'

Dad's eyes almost popped out of his head and
he grabbed Sharon's shoulders. 'What? What did
he say about an Afghan Zebra Hound?'

'Leave me alone, you!' Sharon pulled away

from my dad. 'Everybody knows Charlie's racket, don't they? You must know,' she said, turning to Sergeant Smugg. 'He's your son.'

The sergeant groaned and Sharon went on. 'Charlie's been stealing dogs so that he can pretend to find them and return them to their owners. But then he catches this very special dog, an Afghan Zebra Hound, and he tells me it's really cute and I can have it. I saw it. It was like that mangy mutt you've got there only it had white stripes and longer hair. Well, I don't care how many Zebra Hounds he's got. I hope they all eat him, very slowly, starting with his feet. I've had it with him!' Sharon pulled herself up straight and delivered her parting shot. 'The squirrel,' she declared, 'is history!'

And she stormed out of the police station.

10½. Look Who's in Jail!

'That Charlie of mine . . . he'll be the death of me,' muttered Sergeant Smugg and he picked up the police radio. 'Calling all cars, calling all cars –' He cleared his throat and winced as he spoke the next few words. 'Just look out for my son, Charlie, would you, lads? If you see him bring him in.'

The radio squawked something back at Sergeant Smugg and a scowl clamped on to his face.

'YES! I DID SAY BRING CHARLIE IN! HE'S UNDER ARREST FOR FORGING DOGS!'

He slammed the radio back on the counter. The plastic case shattered and pinged across the room in several different pieces and several different directions. The sergeant picked up the

smashed radio, stared at it and began spluttering incoherently. 'Arghgrrrrsprkkkaaaaghgrrrrh!'

At last he calmed down. He seemed to visibly shrink behind his desk as if all the puff and pride had gone out of him. 'Just wait till I get home. None of this would have happened if only he'd kept his stupid ideas to himself.'

'That's what we thought,' said Tina brightly. 'Although sometimes I think it's not Charlie's ideas that are stupid, it's Charlie himself. Can we go home now?'

'Just a moment,' said Mum, stepping up to Sergeant Smugg's desk. 'I would like to know

how come the triathlon race ended up on the golf
course. That wasn't supposed to happen, was it?'

Sergeant Smugg shook his head. 'I have no
idea.'

One of the police officers was waving his hand
in the air as if he was at school in a maths test.

'I know what happened, Sarge. We – that is
to say – us four constables were on marshalling
duties, directing the cyclists in the right direction,
and then we got the call from you to go to the
golf course at once, so we did. The cyclists must
have taken a wrong turn because we were no

longer directing them and consequently they all ended up at the golf club and, my goodness, didn't we cause a bit of a problem? All that lovely grass churned up and the golf course manager erupting like a volcano. I expect there'll be a lot of fuss about that soon enough.'

'YES! ALL RIGHT! YOU CAN STOP NOW!' yelled Sergeant Smugg. 'And you lot,' he added, pointing at us, 'get out of my police station before I arrest you all for loitering.'

Outside Dad turned and shook hands with us, as if we'd been to court (which we nearly had) and had just won our amazing case against all odds. It felt funny shaking hands with my own father, but I think he was simply pleased that everything had turned out all right.

'So it's like I said, Dad, it wasn't Streaker's fault. It was Charlie's.'

Tina smiled. 'Of course, strictly speaking, it wasn't Charlie who was forging dogs. It was you and me, Trevor.'

'True,' I said. 'But the important thing is that Streaker herself is entirely innocent.'

'Agreed,' said Tina happily.

'Streaker's a good dog at heart.' Dad nodded and patted her. Streaker took hold of his hand. I think she wanted to shake hands with him too, but if you're a dog you can only shake hands with your mouth and Dad thought she was trying to bite him.

'Ow!'

'She's being friendly, Trev's dad,' Tina told him.

'Funny way to be friendly,' my dad muttered.

'So you won't be sending her to boot camp, will you?' I pressed him. There was a bit of a pause, a dangerous moment. It was make-or-break time. What was the answer going to be?

Dad looked hard at Streaker standing there with her tongue hanging out lopsidedly and her ears blasting off frantic 'Aren't-I-A-Good-Dog?' signals.

Dad shook his head. 'No,' he said.

'No?' I repeated. 'What does "no" mean?'

'No, I shan't send her to boot camp,' said Dad, and he smiled.

'But I shan't be giving up golf either, young lady,' he snapped, glaring at Tina. 'So bear that in mind. Not everything has turned out your way.'

We went home a pretty happy bunch. We had to wait to cross the road because a frantic wailing split our eardrums as a police car came hurtling past. Guess who was inside? Charlie Smugg! And he was probably on his way to jail! Bye-bye, Charlie!

Tina and I parted at the corner where our roads met. As I was in the middle of saying cheerio she took me completely by surprise and managed to plant a kiss on my cheek before I'd even finished the *chee* part of cheerio.

Oh well. I didn't mind all that much. Streaker was free and safe and that was the most important thing.

Mum was grinning from ear to ear. 'I'm telling you, Trevor, that girl will have you up the church aisle and with a ring on your finger faster than I can complete a triathlon.'

'Ha ha,' I answered, with as much sarcasm as I could muster. 'And I would like to point out that you never actually completed the triathlon, Mum, and that means there'll never be a ring on my finger.'

Mum laughed and threw an arm round my shoulder. 'All right, you win. Come on, let's go inside. No more triathlons for me! What we need is some chocolate cake and I know just where it is. On the kitchen table! Come on, Streaker, you too! Chocolate cake for everyone. Hooray!'

But there wasn't any chocolate cake on the kitchen table. All we could find were a few crumbs. CRUMBS!

We all turned in the same direction and roared at the tail disappearing out of the back door at a hundred miles an hour.

'STREAKER!!!!'

Jeremy Strong once worked in a bakery, putting the jam into three thousand doughnuts every night. Now he puts the jam in stories instead, which he finds much more exciting. At the age of three, he fell out of a first-floor bedroom window and landed on his head. His mother says that this damaged him for the rest of his life and refuses to take any responsibility. He loves writing stories because he says it is 'the only time you alone have complete control and can make anything happen'. His ambition is to make you laugh (or at least snuffle). Jeremy Strong lives near Bath with his wife, Gillie, three cats and a flying cow.

www.jeremystrong.co.uk

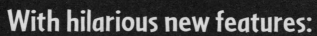

Ask Jeremy

Of all the books you have written, which one is your favourite?

I loved writing both **KRAZY KOW SAVES THE WORLD – WELL, ALMOST** and **STUFF**, my first book for teenagers. Both these made me laugh out loud while I was writing and I was pleased with the overall result in each case. I also love writing the stories about Nicholas and his daft family – **MY DAD**, **MY MUM**, **MY BROTHER** and so on.

If you couldn't be a writer what would you be?

Well, I'd be pretty fed up for a start, because writing was the one thing I knew I wanted to do from the age of nine onward. But if I DID have to do something else, I would love to be either an accomplished pianist or an artist of some sort. Music and art have played a big part in my whole life and I would love to be involved in them in some way.

What's the best thing about writing stories?

Oh dear – so many things to say here! Getting paid for making things up is pretty high on the list! It's also something you do on your own, inside your own head – nobody can interfere with that. The only boss you have is yourself. And you are creating something that nobody else has made before you. I also love making my readers laugh and want to read more and more.

Did you ever have a nightmare teacher?
(And who was your best ever?)

My nightmare at primary school was Mrs Chappell, long since dead. I knew her secret – she was not actually human. She was a Tyrannosaurus rex in disguise. She taught me for two years when I was in Y5 and Y6, and we didn't like each other at all. My best ever was when I was in Y3 and Y4. Her name was Miss Cox, and she was the one who first encouraged me to write stories. She was brilliant. Sadly, she is long dead too.

When you were a kid you used to play kiss-chase. Did you always do the chasing or did anyone ever chase you?!

I usually did the chasing, but when I got chased, I didn't bother to run very fast! Maybe I shouldn't admit to that! We didn't play kiss-chase at school – it was usually played during holidays. If we had tried playing it at school we would have been in serious trouble. Mind you, I seemed to spend most of my time in trouble of one sort or another, so maybe it wouldn't have mattered that much.

LAUGH YOUR SOCKS OFF WITH Jeremy STRONG

Jeremy Strong has written SO many books to make you laugh your socks right off. There are the Streaker books and the Famous Bottom books and the Pyjamas books and ... PHEW!

Welcome to the JEREMY STRONG FAMILY TREE, which shows you all of Jeremy's brilliant books in one easy-to-follow-while-laughing-your-socks-off way!

MY BROTHER'S FAMOUS BOTTOM
Nicholas's baby brother, Cheese, is famous. Well, his bottom is, because he advertises Dumper disposable nappies ...

JOKE BOOKS
You'll never be stuck for a joke to share again.

THE HUNDRED-MILE-AN-HOUR DOG
Streaker is no ordinary dog; she's a rocket on four legs with a woof attached . . .

COSMIC PYJAMAS
Pyjamas are just pyjamas, right? Not when they're COSMIC PYJAMAS, swooooosh! . . .

COWS, CARTOONS, ELEPHANTS AND . . . ORANG-UTANS?!
Warning – may induce red cheeks and tears of laughter!

14½ Things You Didn't Know About

Jeremy Strong

* * * * * * * * * * * * * * * * * * *

1. He loves eating liquorice.

2. He used to like diving. He once dived from the high board and his trunks came off!

3. He used to play electric violin in a rock band called **THE INEDIBLE CHEESE SANDWICH.**

4. He got a 100-metre swimming certificate when he couldn't even swim.

5. When he was five, he sat on a heater and burnt his bottom.

6. Jeremy used to look after a dog that kept eating his underpants. (No – NOT while he was wearing them!)

7. When he was five, he left a basin tap running with the plug in and flooded the bathroom.

8. He can make his ears waggle.

9. He has visited over a thousand schools.

10. He once scored minus ten in an exam! That's ten less than nothing!

11. His hair has gone grey, but his mind hasn't.

12. He'd like to have a pet tiger.

13. He'd like to learn the piano.

14. He has dreadful handwriting.

And a half . . . His favourite hobby is sleeping. He's very good at it.

It all started with a Scarecrow

Puffin is over seventy years old.
Sounds ancient, doesn't it? But Puffin has never been
so lively. We're always on the lookout for the next big
idea, which is how it began all those years ago.

Penguin Books was a big idea from the mind of
a man called Allen Lane, who in 1935 invented
the quality paperback and changed the world.
**And from great Penguins, great Puffins grew,
changing the face of children's books forever.**

The first four Puffin Picture Books were hatched in 1940 and the
first Puffin story book featured a man with broomstick arms called
Worzel Gummidge. In 1967 Kaye Webb, Puffin Editor, started the
Puffin Club, promising to **'make children into readers'**.
She kept that promise and over 200,000 children became devoted
Puffineers through their quarterly instalments of *Puffin Post*.

Many years from now, we hope you'll look back and
remember Puffin with a smile. **No matter what your age
or what you're into, there's a Puffin for everyone.**
The possibilities are endless, but one thing is for sure:
whether it's a picture book or a paperback, a sticker book
or a hardback, **if it's got that little Puffin
on it – it's bound to be good.**

www.puffin.co.uk

Your story starts here . . .

Do you **love books** and
discovering new stories?
Then **www.puffin.co.uk**
is the place for you . . .

• Thrilling adventures, fantastic fiction
and laugh-out-loud fun

• Brilliant videos featuring your favourite authors
and characters

• Exciting competitions, news, activities,
the Puffin blog and SO MUCH more . . .

www.puffin.co.uk